An Ashanti Tale

Oh, Kojo! How Could You!

retold by VERNA AARDEMA
Pictures by MARC BROWN

Dial Books for Young Readers
New York

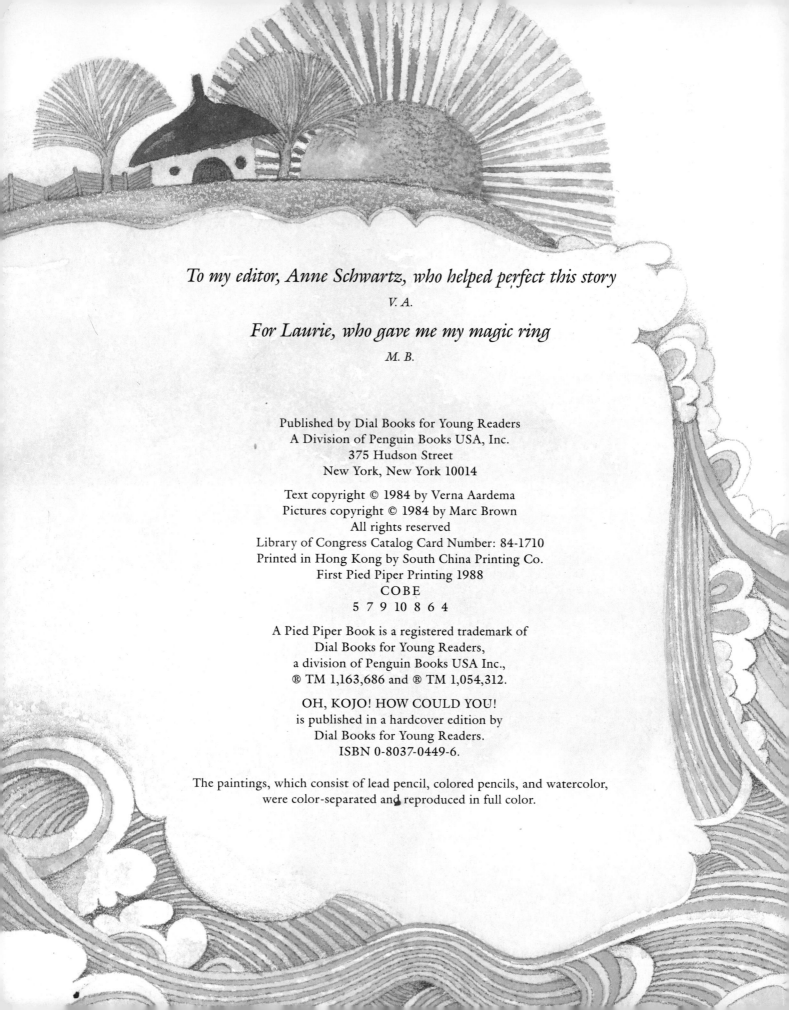

To my editor, Anne Schwartz, who helped perfect this story
V. A.

For Laurie, who gave me my magic ring
M. B.

Published by Dial Books for Young Readers
A Division of Penguin Books USA, Inc.
375 Hudson Street
New York, New York 10014

Text copyright © 1984 by Verna Aardema
Pictures copyright © 1984 by Marc Brown
All rights reserved
Library of Congress Catalog Card Number: 84-1710
Printed in Hong Kong by South China Printing Co.
First Pied Piper Printing 1988
COBE
5 7 9 10 8 6 4

A Pied Piper Book is a registered trademark of
Dial Books for Young Readers,
a division of Penguin Books USA Inc.,
® TM 1,163,686 and ® TM 1,054,312.

OH, KOJO! HOW COULD YOU!
is published in a hardcover edition by
Dial Books for Young Readers.
ISBN 0-8037-0449-6.

The paintings, which consist of lead pencil, colored pencils, and watercolor,
were color-separated and reproduced in full color.

In Ashantiland, in the old days, whenever mischief was done, people would always say: It isn't one thing. It isn't two things. It's Ananse!

Ananse lived beside the path that crosses the River-that-Gurgles-*PonponponPONsa*. Across the river was the hut of a woman named Tutuola. She lived by herself and was very lonely.

One Monday Tutuola went to the River-that-Gurgles-*PonponponPONsa*. She said, "Spirit of the River, give me a son."

The River Spirit answered in a gurgly voice, "You shall have a son. But he will not like to work. He will only like to spend your money. However, one day he will repay you."

Tutuola went home. And that very afternoon, she had a son. She named him Kojo, which is the usual name for a son who is born on Monday. Since he was a magic child, he was not long in growing up. By evening he had become a young man.

The next morning, as soon as dawn lighted the doorway, Kojo said, "Ma, give me a packet of gold dust. I want to go to the sea to buy salt."

Tutuola said to herself, "It is just as the River Spirit said—he only wants to spend money!" But she gave him an Asuanu of gold dust. And she warned him, "Have nothing to do with that trickster, Ananse, who lives beyond the river."

Kojo set out. Soon he came to the River-that-Gurgles-*Ponpon-ponPONsa*. The water was only knee-deep, so he splashed through it, *che-a, che-a, che-a*.

Farther on Kojo saw the compound of Ananse. The man was sitting in his doorway with a small pile of sticks in front of him.

Now, Kojo had meant to pass by Ananse's house without even saying *how-do*. But just then a dog ran to Ananse with a stick in his mouth. And, TIK, he dropped it on the pile.

Kojo heard Ananse say, "Good dog. Now fetch another one." The dog trotted into the bushes and came back with another stick.

What Kojo didn't know was that this was a game Ananse played with his dog. He would throw a whole armful of sticks and wait for the dog to retrieve them.

Kojo asked, "Ananse, is that dog gathering firewood?"

Ananse chuckled, *gug, gug, gug*. He saw the gold in Kojo's hand, and a greedy gleam came into his eyes. He said, "This here dog is an African Wood Hound. He gathers wood all by himself."

Now, Kojo didn't like to work. And he thought it would be a great convenience to have a dog that fetched firewood. He asked, "Ananse, will you sell that dog?"

Ananse was willing. And soon he had the gold. And Kojo had the dog!

When Tutuola saw what he had bought, she said, "Oh, Kojo! How could you! A whole packet of gold dust for one good-for-nothing dog!"

And when she found that the only wood the dog would fetch was the stick thrown for him, she knew that indeed Kojo had been tricked. Tutuola said, "It isn't one thing. It isn't two things. It's Ananse! Kojo, did you buy that dog from Ananse?"

Kojo had to admit that he had.

Market Day came round, and as soon as dawn lighted the doorway, Kojo said, "Ma, give me a packet of gold dust. I want to go to market to buy cloth."

Tutuola said, "You will only throw the money away again!" But Kojo begged and begged. And at last Tutuola gave in.

Kojo set out. Soon he reached the River-that-Gurgles-*Ponpon-ponPONsa*. He splashed through it, *che-a, che-a, che-a*.

Farther on, as he was passing Ananse's house, Kojo saw a rat scurry, RASS, across the yard. A cat went after it, *kpata, kpata, kpata*. Soon she returned with the rat in her mouth.

What Kojo didn't know was that this was a game Ananse played with his cat and his pet rat. Kojo thought if he had that cat, he would never have to sleep in fear of rats again. He asked, "Ananse, will you sell that cat?"

Ananse was willing. And soon he had the gold. And Kojo had the cat!

When Tutuola saw what he had bought, she cried, "Oh, Kojo! How could you! A whole packet of gold dust for one good-for-nothing cat!" Then she threw up her hands and said, "It isn't one thing. It isn't two things. It's Ananse! Kojo, did you buy that cat from Ananse?"

And Kojo had to admit that he had.

The next Market Day, as soon as dawn lighted the doorway, Kojo said, "Ma, give me a packet of gold dust. I want to go to market to buy tools."

Tutuola said, "You will only throw the money away again!"

"No-o, Ma," said Kojo. "This time I won't stop at Ananse's house. I won't even look at it!"

So Tutuola gave him the money. And he set out. However, before he reached the river, whom should he meet but Ananse!

Ananse had a dove on a string. The dove was scratching in the leaves beside the path. She found a snail and dropped it, PIP, into a basket that Ananse carried. She found another snail and another.

Now, Kojo liked fried snails past all things. But he didn't like to hunt for them. He asked, "Ananse, will you sell that dove?"

Ananse was willing. And soon he had the gold. And Kojo had the dove.

When Tutuola saw what he had bought, she cried, "Oh, Kojo! How could you! A whole packet of gold dust for one good-for-nothing dove!"

At that the dove began to moan, *koo-wee-oo, koo-wee-oo.* "In my country I was the Queen Mother," she sobbed. "Ananse caught me and made me his slave. Please take me back to my people."

Kojo said, "Then I would have nothing!"

"My son is the chief," said the dove. "He will reward you."

Kojo laughed, *tu-e, tu-e, tu-e.* "Ma," he said, "maybe this dove is not such a bad bargain after all."

The next day, as soon as dawn lighted the doorway, Kojo carried the dove back to her kingdom. When they arrived, hundreds of doves flocked about them, calling, *a-koo, a-koo, a-koo*.

The dove chief was so happy to see his mother safely returned, he gave Kojo a magic ring.

When Tutuola saw the magic ring, she cried, "Oh, Kojo! How could you be so lucky! Ai! The River Spirit said you would repay me!"

"Wait," said Kojo, "let us see if the magic works." He held up the ring and said, "Magic Ring, make us a village."

At once a wide circle of houses appeared. Kojo and Tutuola named the village Wa, which means *Come*. Many people came to live in the village. Kojo became the chief, or Na, of Wa. Tutuola became the Queen Mother. And the dog and cat lived with them in the royal compound.

Another day Kojo said, "Magic Ring, make cows and goats for my people, and for me all the fine things a great chief needs." The animals and the things appeared, even a talking drum and a drummer to play it.

Now, Ananse heard that Kojo had become a rich chief through the power of a magic ring—a ring he had obtained in exchange for *his* dove. He said, "Yo! That ring should be mine!" And he sent his beautiful young niece to steal it.

The girl put on a new cloth and her best ornaments. When he saw her, Kojo was charmed. He showed her all his fine things—including the magic ring.

"Na of Wa," said the niece, "what I have heard about you is indeed true. Now I shall go back and tell my people."

She pretended to go away, but instead she hid nearby in the forest. When she saw Kojo go to the river to bathe, she went into his house. She found the magic ring, and she took it to Ananse!

Upon his return Kojo discovered that the ring was gone. He went to the River-that-Gurgles-*PonponponPONsa*. He said, "Spirit of the River, someone has stolen my magic ring."

The River Spirit answered in a gurgly voice, "It isn't one thing. It isn't two things. It's Ananse! He has your ring in a box in the middle of all his boxes."

"How can I get it back?" asked Kojo.

"Send your cat and dog to get it," said the River Spirit. "Tell them not to eat anything along the way. Ananse will try to poison them."

So Kojo sent his cat and dog to get the ring, and he warned them not to eat anything they found on the path.

The two set out, with the cat running ahead. Soon they came to the River-that-Gurgles-*PonponponPONsa*. The cat said, "Dog, please carry me across. I can't swim!"

But the dog snapped, "Too bad for you! You will just have to walk across on the river bottom." So the cat held her breath and did that, while the dog swam on the surface, *freh, freh, freh.*

Beyond the river the cat again ran ahead. She came to a piece of meat, leaped over it, and went on. But when the dog saw the meat, he ate it, *t-lop, t-lop*. At once he fell into a deep sleep.

Upon reaching Ananse's house the cat found the man napping on his mat. Quietly she crept past him and up to the rafters where the boxes were kept. She opened the middle box, took out the ring, and stole away with it in her teeth.

Back on the path the cat came upon the sleeping dog, "Wake up!" she cried. "I have the ring."

The dog stretched and yawned, EE-AH! Then he ran along behind the cat. When they arrived home, the cat told how the dog had refused to carry her across the river, and how he had eaten the poison meat and had not helped at all!

"You good-for-nothing dog!" cried Kojo. "From this day you shall sleep outdoors. And when I feed you, I will throw your food upon the ground!"

"As for you, Cat," he said, "when I sleep, you shall sleep on a corner of my mat. And when I eat, I shall put a little of my food in a dish for you."

And to this day in Ashantiland cats get better care than dogs. People are remembering the dog who did not help at all and the cat who helped a young chief get the better of Ananse.